Hugo
at the
Window

Anne Rockwell

Macmillan Publishing Company   New York

Collier Macmillan Publishers   London

Printed and bound in Japan. First American Edition

10   9   8   7   6   5   4   3   2   1

The text of this book is set in 20 point ITC Newtext Book. The illustrations are rendered in pen and ink and watercolor on paper.
Library of Congress Cataloging-in-Publication Data   Rockwell, Anne F.   Hugo at the window.   Summary: A dog waits and waits at the window for his friend who is gone a long time, but there is a surprise for Hugo when his friend returns. [1. Dogs—Fiction. 2. Birthdays—Fiction] I. Title.   PZ7.R5943Hu   1988   [E]   87-11058
ISBN 0-02-777330-2

This is Hugo.

This is his friend.

They live on the second floor

in a red brick building.

One day Hugo's friend
went somewhere,
but Hugo had to stay home.
"I'll be back soon,"
said Hugo's friend.

Hugo looked out the window,
watching and waiting.
But his friend
did not come back.
Where did he go?

Bakery

BUS
STOP

KNIT SHOP

PET STORE

Hugo looked out the window,
watching and waiting
some more.
But still his friend
did not come back.
Where did he go?

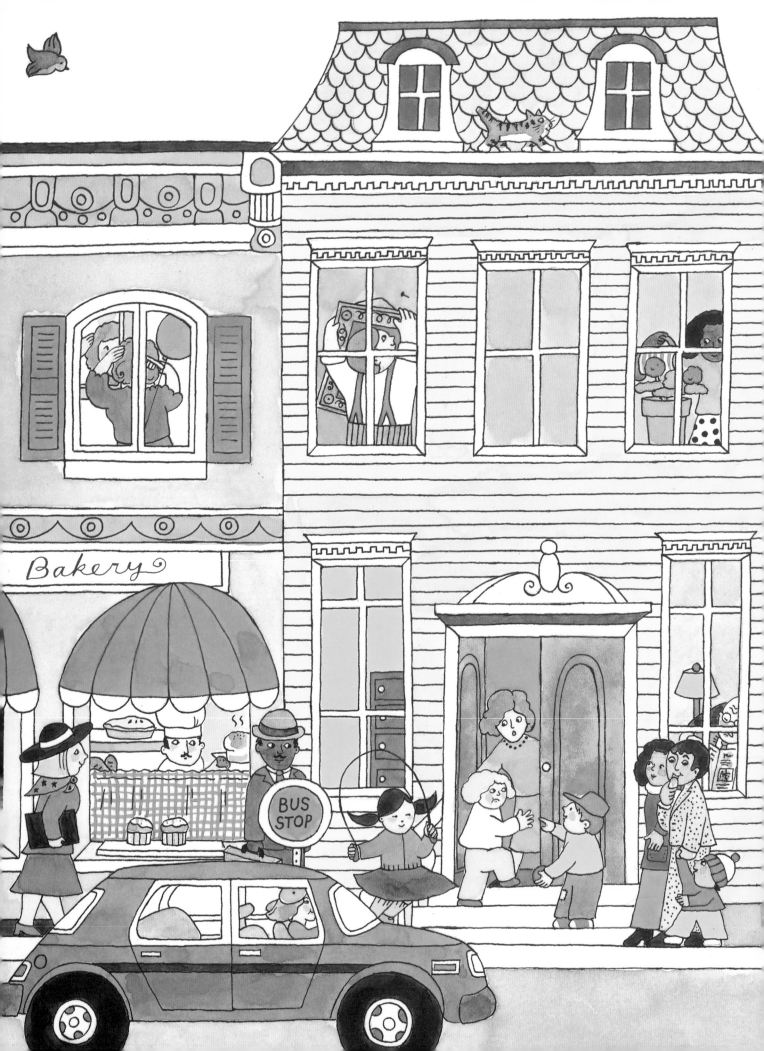

Bakery

BUS
STOP

KNIT SHOP

PET STORE

Hugo stayed at the window.

He went on watching and waiting.

But his friend

did not come back.

Why had he left

poor Hugo all alone?

Where did his friend go?

Bakery

KNIT
SHOP

PET STORE

Hugo felt very sad.
He wanted his friend
to come back to him.

Bakery

BUS
STOP

KNIT
SHOP

PET STORE

Finally Hugo got tired
of looking out the window,
watching and waiting.
He lay on the floor,
listening at the door
and feeling very lonely.

Then Hugo's friend came back!
He had company for Hugo
and presents for Hugo
and cupcakes for Hugo
because it was Hugo's birthday.

Everyone sat down
and sang
"Happy Birthday to Hugo"
and blew out the candles
and ate Hugo's cupcakes.

After the party they all went
for a walk down the street.

Hugo wore his new red sweater
and carried his new rubber bone.

Hugo was very, very happy.